Little Charmers

SANTA SPARKLE

Adapted by Meredith Rusu
from the teleplay by John May and Suzanne Bolch

Published by Scholastic Inc., *Publishers since 1920.* SCHOLASTIC and associated logos are trademarks and/or registered trademarks of Scholastic Inc.

The publisher does not have any control over and does not assume any responsibility for author or third-party websites or their content.

ISBN 978-1-338-09764-1

10 9 8 7 6 5 4 3 2 1   16 17 18 19 20
                                             40
Printed in the U.S.A.
First printing 2016
Book design by Erin McMahon and Becky James

SCHOLASTIC INC.

It was Sparkle Night in Charmville, and the three Little Charmers were bursting with holiday spirit. Especially Hazel!

"I can't wait to see who will place the Sparkle Star on top of the tree this year!" she told her friends.

"Well, you won't have to wait long," said Lavender. "The tree decorating ceremony is about to start. Let's go!"

In a swirl of shimmer and snow, the Charmers flew on their brooms to the town square.

Everyone in Charmville was already gathered around the beautiful Sparkle Night tree.

Each year, the Charmer who had shown the most Sparkle Spirit all season long was chosen to place the star at the very top.

Secretly, Hazel hoped it would be her!

She snapped a quick photo with her magic camera.

"This is definitely going in my Sparkle Night album," she told her friends. "I never want to forget this night!"

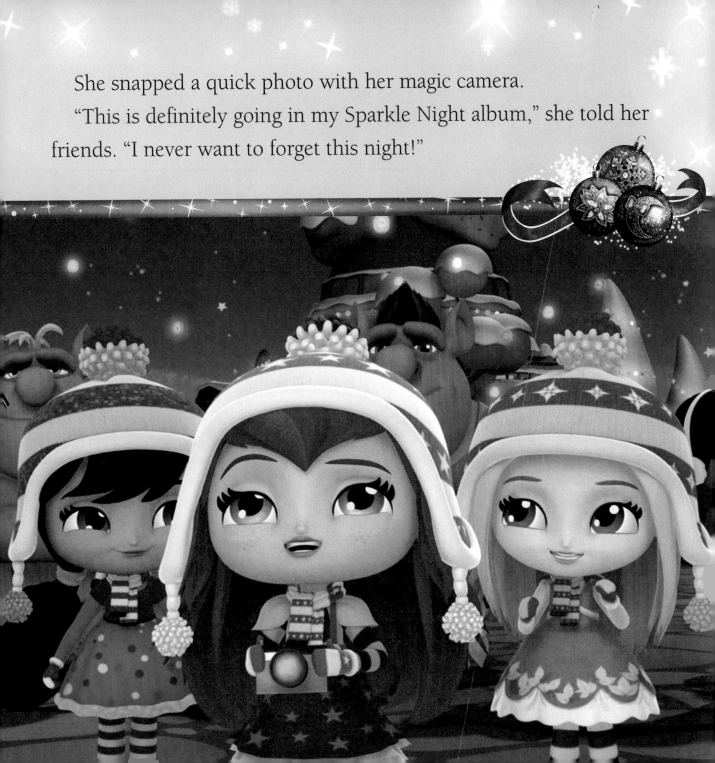

Just then, Hazel's mom arrived. She had a magic envelope. And beside her floated a velvet pillow carrying the shimmering Sparkle Star.

"This year, the chosen Charmer is . . ."

She read from the envelope. "My daughter, Hazel Charming!"

Hazel gasped. She *had* been chosen!

"I can't miss this moment!" she exclaimed.

With a wave of her wand, Hazel cast a picture-taking charm.

"Magic camera, make like an elfie, and take me a charmtastic selfie!"

But Hazel's charm misfired.

Zip! Zap! Zoom!

It whizzed past the camera . . . bounced off a lamp post . . . and broke the Sparkle Star!

The crowd gasped. Everyone knew a broken Sparkle Star was almost impossible to fix.

"It's okay, Hazel," her mom said. "It was an accident."

But Hazel was heartbroken. "I've ruined Sparkle Night for everyone."

That night, Hazel couldn't sleep.

"How can I fix the Sparkle Star?" she asked her cat, Seven. "I need the help of a super-strong Charmer. Someone like . . . Santa Sparkle! He's the magic-est Charmer there is!"

Quick as a fairy wink, Hazel called her friends.

Together, they waited for Santa Sparkle to come down the chimney.

"Do you really think he can fix the star?" Posie asked.

Suddenly, the Charmers heard a rustling on the rooftop.

Could it be?

"Ho, ho, ho!" Santa Sparkle came tumbling down the chimney!

"It's him!" cried Hazel. "I *need* a picture of this!"

"Magic camera, head over yonder.
Take a picture, it lasts longer!"

Snapdragons! Hazel's charm backfired again. It shot up the chimney and busted Santa's sleigh in two. And then . . . it turned Santa Sparkle into a Santa mouse!

"Did what I think just happened *actually* just happen?" asked Lavender.

"Oh, no!" cried Hazel. "I've turned Santa Sparkle into a Santa mouse! Quick, we have to spell him back, or no one in Charmville will get presents, and then Sparkle Night will *really* be ruined!"

Posie and Lavender nodded. "It's time to Santa Sparkle up!"

The friends flew to the Charmhouse and cast their most powerful spell yet.

"The real Santa Sparkle wasn't tiny, was he? So, come on, play along, don't be small and fuzzy!"

Poof! The spell worked!

"Ho, ho, ho! Thanks for that!" said Santa Sparkle. "What happened? One second we were taking a picture, and the next, I really wanted a piece of cheese!"

"It was my fault," admitted Hazel. "I got carried away."

"But it's okay now," said Lavender. "Everything's back to normal."

"Well, not everything." Santa Sparkle pointed out the window. "There's still the little matter of my sleigh."

"Uh-oh," groaned Lavender. "I don't know if we have a magic fix for that."

But a gleam came to Hazel's eye. "I think I know one person who might."

There was only one Wizard mechanic whizzy enough to fix Santa Sparkle's sleigh.

Hazel's dad!

"Hmmm," he said when he saw the damage. "It looks like Hazel's charm took the zoom out of the zoom-ma-mater! My magic brooms can power it. But we're going to need to work as a team to get it going!"

"Okay, Charmers, wands up!" he said. "Give it everything you've got!"

With all their Sparkle Night might, the Charmers and Hazel's dad charmed Santa's sleigh until . . .

Pop! It snapped back together, ready to fly!

"Thank you, Dad!" cried Hazel. "You're the best."

Then Hazel turned to Santa Sparkle. "It's getting late. I'm sorry for all the trouble I caused. You should probably get going."

"You know, Little Charmer," said Santa Sparkle. "I've been around awhile. And I know that trouble comes in threes. Is there something else that needs fixing?"

Hazel took Santa Sparkle to see the broken Sparkle Star.

He cast a powerful spell. But even his magic wasn't strong enough
to fix it.

"It's okay," Hazel said sadly. "I know you have to get going. You
have a lot of people depending on you to deliver presents. Not
just me."

Suddenly, the Sparkle Star began twinkling. In a burst of light, it became whole again!

"You did it!" cried Hazel.

"No, Little Charmer," Santa Sparkle told her. "*You* did it. Because you put others before yourself. And that's what the magic of Sparkle Night is all about."

With a wave of his wand, Santa Sparkle made three colorful stars to go alongside the Sparkle Star. The Charmers and Hazel's dad put them at the very top of the tree.

"Ho, ho, ho! Charmazing!" cried Santa Sparkle. "And now, since I am running behind, there is one other thing I could use your help with, Little Charmers . . ."

Much later that night, long after all of Charmville had fallen fast asleep, a magical sight flew through the sky. It was Santa Sparkle in his sleigh, followed by three very special Sparkle Elves.

"Happy Sparkle Night, everybody!"